JUDITH CASELEY

GREENWILLOW BOOKS New York

Watercolor paints and colored pencils were used for the full-color art.
The text type is Avant Garde Medium and Veljovic Book.

Library of Congress Cataloging-in-Publication Data

Caseley, Judith.
Dear Annie / by Judith Caseley.
p.   cm.
Summary: Presents a series of postcards and
letters Annie sends to or receives from her
loving grandfather from the time she is born.
ISBN 0-688-10010-4. ISBN 0-688-10011-2 (lib. bdg.)
[1. Grandfathers—Fiction.   2. Letters.]   I. Title.
PZ7.C2677De   1991
[E]—dc20
90-39793   CIP   AC

To my mother and father

Grandpa's first letter to Annie when she was born
had a picture of a rose on the front of it.
Grandpa wrote:

Dearest Annie,
    Welcome to this world. When I saw you
for the first time through the window at the
hospital, you looked like a rose. That's why
I chose this card.
                              Love,
                              Grandpa

Mama read it to Annie in her cradle. Mama wrote back:

Dear Dad,

Annie <u>is</u> like a little flower, with her pink cheeks and rosebud mouth. She cries quite a lot, but we love her.

Love,

Catherine

Then she strapped Annie in a little pouch, and they mailed the postcard together.

When Annie was one, Grandpa sent her a birthday letter. It said:

> We hear you are walking now. Soon we can go hiking in the woods together, and we can look for bear tracks. The bluejay in this picture is exactly the color of your eyes.
>
> I love you,
> Grandpa

Mama wrote back:

Dear Dad,
    She'll be dancing soon! She rocks back and
forth in her high chair when I have the radio on.
She's a wonder. We'll visit in a few weeks.
        Love,
        Catherine

Then she walked to the mailbox with Annie, and she
lifted Annie up, and Annie put the letter in the mailbox.

When Annie was two, Grandpa wrote:

I just received your lovely picture. The mailman rang my bell and said, "Looks like a special letter." And there it was—your drawing of Shermie the cat. We had a dog named Buster when I was little. My mother gave him away because she said he ate too much. I was sad for a long time.

Love,
Grandpa

P.S. I am sending you this card because I imagine when you get older you might look a little like the girl in this picture, who is French and called Mathilde.

Mama wrote back:

Dear Dad,

Annie liked the picture of Mathilde so much that she called her new doll Mathilde. "What's her name again?" she says when she picks up her doll. We'll visit next week. Annie says I should tell you to get her some books from the library.

When Annie was older, she visited Grandpa.
Grandpa took her on her first sleigh ride, and they
went ice-skating, too. When Annie told Grandpa good-
bye, she said, "Now you can write me my letter."

Annie went home and waited.

"Mail doesn't come at night," said her mother.

The next day Annie waited some more.
She sat on the steps, listening for the
click of the mailbox.
"Mail doesn't come on Sunday, either,"
said her mother.

Finally a letter from Grandpa arrived. It said:

Here is a picture of skaters on a pond in winter. It reminds me of McGilvray's Pond and how much fun we had skating. And you just laughed when you fell down!
I had hot chocolate again today.
It tasted better when you were here.

Annie dictated to her mother:

Dear Grandpa,

Today I watched a tape about a little mermaid. She swam a lot. Mama says in the summertime you'll take me swimming. I'll be the mermaid.

And Grandpa wrote back to Annie:

Dear Annie Mermaid,

  Of course we'll go swimming. I'm glad you enjoyed the tape. When I was a small boy, we had no VCR, no television, and no computers. But I had lots of books and loved to go to the library.

Annie wrote back with her mother:

Dear Grandpa,

    Tapes are fun, but I go to the library, too. I like books on witches and babies. Sometimes the witches are scary, but the babies aren't.

This time, while Mama sat on the bench,
Annie mailed the card all by herself.

A few months later Grandpa wrote:

I enjoyed your dancing so much at Grandma's birthday party. Here is a picture of a famous ballerina named Anna Pavlova. She came from Russia, where your ancestors came from almost a hundred years ago. She even has your name.

Annie wrote back, all by herself:

Dear Grandpa,
    Mama took me to ballet class. I liked it,
except when the teacher pushed on my
knees. It hurt.

Grandpa wrote back:

Dearest Annie,

I never danced much when I was young.
This man, Henry VIII, was the king of England
five hundred years ago. He was very stout
and a fine wrestler. I used to wrestle in college,
and so did your Uncle Larry. Sometimes it hurt,
too, but mostly I liked it. I'm going to
the post office to mail this card sending
you all my love.

The weeks and months passed.
Annie saved every one of Grandpa's cards and
letters in a shoebox that she decorated herself.

One day Annie brought her box of letters to school for show-and-tell. When it was her turn, she stood up in front of the class.

"My grandpa is my pen pal," she said. "So far I have 86 cards and letters from him. I write back to him, too, and then every day I wait for the mail."

Annie sat down. The teacher
passed around Annie's
box of letters. The children
liked it better than Roy's robot or
Cornelia's celebrity microphone
or even Mindy's Sweet Shoppe
with the tiny ice cream sodas.

They decided they wanted to have
pen pals, too.

The class made a bulletin board called Mail from Everybody. Soon there were cards and letters from all over the world in all sorts of handwriting.

Annie put a few of Grandpa's postcards on the board, but just a few. She kept most of them for herself, because they were special.

Nobody has as many letters as Annie. Over a hundred
now. And Grandpa keeps sending them, every week.